JUV/E8
FIC
MAYER

EASTSI

W9-CLX-442

R0404772310

Snow day

A NOTE TO PARENTS

Congratulations on choosing the best in educational materials for your child. By selecting top-quality McGraw-Hill products, you can be assured that the concepts used in our books will reinforce and enhance the skills that are being taught in classrooms nationwide.

And what better way to get young readers excited than with Mercer Mayer's Little Critter, a character loved by children everywhere? Our First Readers offer simple and engaging stories about Little Critter that children can read on their own. Each level incorporates reading skills, colorful illustrations, and challenging activities.

Level 1 – The stories are simple and use repetitive language. Illustrations are highly supportive.
Level 2 - The stories begin to grow in complexity. Language is still repetitive, but it is mixed with more challenging vocabulary.
Level 3 - The stories are more complex. Sentences are longer and more varied.

To help your child make the most of this book, look at the first few pictures in the story and discuss what is happening. Ask your child to predict where the story is going. Then, once your child has read the story, have him or her review the word list and do the activities. This will reinforce vocabulary words from the story and build reading comprehension.

You are your child's first and most influential teacher. No one knows your child the way you do. Tailor your time together to reinforce a newly acquired skill or to overcome a temporary stumbling block. Praise your child's progress and ideas, take delight in his or her imagination, and most of all, enjoy your time together!

Library of Congress Cataloging-in-Publication Data

Mayer, Mercer, 1943-
    Snow day / by Mercer Mayer.
        p. cm. – (First readers, skills and practice)
    Summary: Little Critter explores some of the fun things he can do when school is cancelled because of
the snow. Includes activities.
    PB ISBN 1-57768-805-8
    HC ISBN 1-57768-457-5
        [1. Snow—Fiction.] I. Title. II. Series.

PZ7.M462 Sn 2001
[E]—dc21   2001031208

 # Children's Publishing

Text Copyright © 2002 McGraw-Hill Children's Publishing.
Art Copyright © 2002 Mercer Mayer.

All rights reserved. Except as permitted under the United States Copyright Act, no part of this
publication may be reproduced or distributed in any form or by any means, or stored in a
database retrieval system, without prior written permission from the publisher, unless
otherwise indicated.
LITTLE CRITTER, MERCER MAYER'S LITTLE CRITTER and MERCER MAYER'S LITTLE CRITTER
logo are registered trademarks of Orchard House Licensing Company. All rights reserved.

Send all inquiries to:
McGraw-Hill Children's Publishing
8787 Orion Place
Columbus, OH 43240-4027

Printed in the United States of America.
PB 1-57768-805-8
HC 1-57768-457-5

1 2 3 4 5 6 7 8 9 10 PHXBK 06 05 04 03 02

 A Big Tuna Trading Company, LLC/J. R. Sansevere Book

The **McGraw·Hill** Companies

EAS

FIRST READERS

Level 1   Grades PreK–K

SNOW DAY

by Mercer Mayer

Mc
Graw
Hill **Children's Publishing**

Columbus, Ohio

Chicago Public Library
Vodak/East Side Branch
3710 E. 106th St.
Chicago, IL 60617

Today is a snow day.
There is no school.
What can I do?

R0404772310

5

I can catch
snowflakes.

I can make
a snowman.

I can make a snow fort.

I can make
snowballs.

13

I am getting cold!

I can make myself warm.

16

17

Word List

Read each word in the lists below. Then, find each word in the story. Now, make up a new sentence using the word. Say your sentence out loud.

Words I Know
snow
school
snowflakes
snowman
snow fort
snowballs

Challenge Words
today
catch
myself
warm

Words and Letters

Read the story again. Point to each word as you read.

Go to page 7. How many words are on page 7?

Turn to page 8. Point to a word that has 3

letters in it.

Which words on page 8 have only one letter?

What is the 2nd word on page 10?

Matching

Match the correct pairs of mittens and gloves.

Left to Right

Use your finger to trace the dotted line in each picture. Move from left to right.

End Punctuation

A period tells you that it is time to stop at the end of a sentence. How many periods are in the story?

.
This is a period.

A question mark tells you that someone is asking a question. How many question marks are in the story?

?
This is a question mark.

An exclamation point tells you that someone is very excited. How many exclamation points are in the story?

!
This is an exclamation point.

22

Logical Reasoning

It's winter. Point to the things Little Critter needs to wear when he goes outside on a snowy day.

Answer Key

page 19
Words and Letters

Read the story again. Point to each word as you read.

Go to page 7. How many words are on page 7?
_____4_____

Turn to page 8. Find a word that has 3 letters in it? Write the word here: _____can_____

What words on page 8 have only one letter?
_____I_____ and _____a_____

What is the 2nd word on page 10?
_____can_____

page 20
Matching

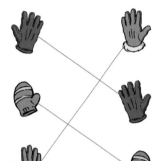

page 21
Left to Right

page 22
End Punctuation

A period tells you that it is time to stop at the end of a sentence. How many periods are in the story?
_____7_____

This is a period.

?
This is a question mark.

A question mark tells you that someone is asking a question. How many question marks are in the story? _____1_____

An exclamation point tells you that someone is very excited. How many exclamation points are in the story? _____1_____

!
This is an exclamation point.

page 23
Logical Reasoning

24